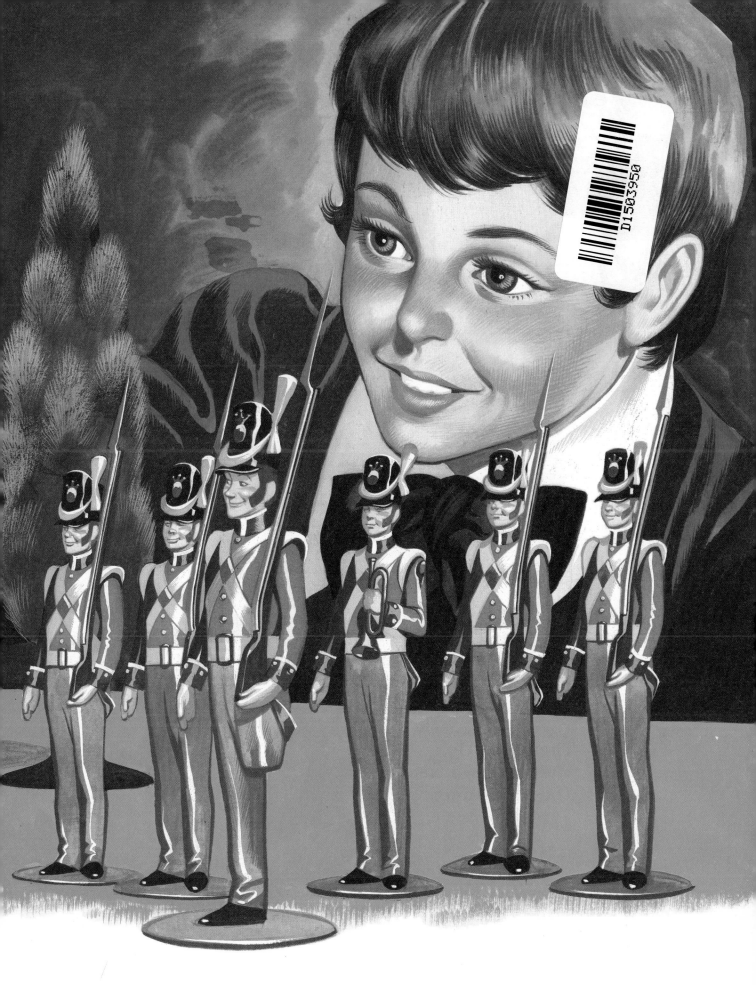

3

Contents

Published in this edition by Galley Press, an imprint of
W.H. Smith and Son Limited. Registered No. 237811 England.
Trading as WHS Distributors, St John's House, East Street, Leicester, LE1 6NE.
Copyright © Art Work and text produced by Martspress Limited. 23 Nork Way,
Banstead, Surrey, SM7 1PB. 1985 in association with Patrick Hawkey & Co. Ltd.

ISBN 0 86136 783 9

Printed and bound by Brepols N.V. – Turnhout, Belgium

The Little Tin Soldier
and other stories

Stories adapted by Barbara Hayes
Illustrated by Ronald and Gerry Embleton

✸ The Little Tin Soldier ✸

Once upon a time a box of twenty-five toy soldiers was bought for a young boy. The soldiers were lined up in a long row and carried muskets over their shoulders and wore grand uniforms and were a fine, brave-looking body of men.

The last soldier in the row had only one leg. The elderly toymaker had, most

unfortunately, run out of metal when he came to this last tin soldier and had put him into the box unfinished.

This brave tin soldier was not one to complain. He knew soldiers should be full of courage so he stood up straight and firm on his one leg and made up his mind his master would be proud of him.

There were other toys in the playroom where the box of soldiers lived.

One was a beautiful dancer. She stood poised on one leg in the doorway of the fine toy castle. Her other leg was tucked up under her pretty dress. The steadfast tin soldier did not know this. He considered the beautiful dancer was just like him – one-legged.

"That lovely girl would make a suitable wife for me," he decided.

Then he looked at the castle in which the dancer lived and said to himself: "If she is used to living in a castle, she would not be content to come and live in a box. In any case, there is not enough space for an extra person."

However, he was forced to think of the Jack-in-the-box, who was an unpleasant fellow forever jeering at the other toys.

One day, after the tin soldier and the Jack-in-the-box had exchanged some cross words, the boy put the tin soldier on to the ledge in front of the window.

The little tin soldier held his musket firmly on his shoulder. He stood steadily on his one leg. He looked straight ahead without blinking. He guarded the window well, as a brave soldier should.

He thought of the evening before. If only the boy knew what went on in the toyroom after dark, how surprised he would be.

As soon as their young master and his brothers and sisters were tucked up to sleep, the toys came to life.

Twenty-four of the toy soldiers lined up and marched up and down.

Left-right! Left-right!

They drilled and paraded like the best soldiers of the king.

The little tin soldier with the one leg could not march with the others, but he stood brave and firm with no sign of sorrow on his face.

"If I cannot march, then I will be steadfast and true," he smiled.

The dolls went to tea with each other. The toy nurses and doctors pretended to work in their hospital. The crayons climbed out of their packets and turned the pages of the colouring books. The toy oven glowed and cooked tiny cakes for the little folk who lived in the doll's house.

"Am I the only person not to move and join in the jollity?" thought the tin soldier, but never for a single moment did he cease standing smartly at attention and shouldering his musket and staring boldly to the front.

Then he noticed that the beautiful dancer was not moving either.

She stood always delicately balanced on her one long leg, her graceful arms held up high, her lovely dress shining in the evening light and her other leg tucked out of sight under the frills of her skirt.

"We are so alike," thought the tin soldier. "I'm sure we were meant for each other." But neither of them moved.

Then that evening, as on every evening, the clock struck twelve. CRASH!

The lid of the Jack-in-the-box sprang open and the sneering Jack-in-the-box came leaping out, looking for trouble.

He glared angrily at the dolls and the doctors and nurses, but they were too busy to take any notice of him.

He scowled at the soldiers, but they were on the battlements of the castle preparing to fire a cannon and he dared not jeer at them.

Then he bent over the lone tin soldier standing steadfast and firm on his one leg.

"What are you staring at?" snapped the Jack-in-the-box.

The tin soldier looked straight forward and did not reply.

Soldiers on duty are not supposed to chatter to strangers.

"I'll teach you to stare at me," snarled the Jack-in-the-box. "You should keep

your eyes to yourself. I will make trouble for you tomorrow."

Then he turned to shout hurtful things at the other toys.

The night sped by. At last the toys became tired and settled back into their homes and went to sleep.

Next morning, the sun had risen and the tin soldier was standing on the window ledge, thinking about the Jack-in-the-box. "He cannot harm me," thought the tin soldier, but he was wrong.

The Jack-in-the-box was in possession of magic powers. He made the boy think it would be nice to open the window in front of the toy soldier. Then he made the boy

think it would be fun to stand the Jack-in-the-box in the fresh air outside.

CRASH!

The lid of the box flew back and the Jack-in-the-box sprang out.

His arms flapped wide and his hands cut through the air. They knocked the little tin soldier off balance. He fell off the window ledge, through the air and down, down into the street below. How the Jack-in-the-box laughed.

It was a long fall from the window to the ground. The tin soldier rolled over and over until he hit the stone sidewalk.

He bounced and rolled and twisted until he came to rest, far along the road,

standing upside down with his bayonet caught in a crack between the cobbles.

Still the steadfast little tin soldier did not cry out or complain. He stood to attention and stared forward with a brave face, as a soldier should.

The little boy was very upset.

He called the maidservant and the two of them ran down to the road.

They searched the pavements and the cobbled road and peered into the muddy puddles, but they could not see the tin soldier.

He had bounced far away from their door and they were not looking for him in the right place.

"Tin soldier! Tin soldier! Where are you?" called the boy.

The tin soldier stood to attention but the wet and the cold made his lips so stiff he could not reply.

It was windy and raining and the maidservant wanted to go back indoors.

"We cannot stay out here, young master," she said to the boy. "You are getting soaked. Mistress will be cross with me if you catch cold."

"But the soldier must be around here somewhere," wailed the boy.

"That may be," replied the maidservant, "but we cannot see him. In any case it was only that soldier with one leg, wasn't it? Losing him does not matter. You can play with the twenty-four other good soldiers."

The boy sighed and after one last look round the street, he went back indoors.

"I know he had only one leg," said the boy as they mounted the stairs back to the playroom, "but he stood straight and true and I am sure he had a brave and faithful heart."

The steadfast tin soldier just managed to hear the boy's words. He felt so proud! But now, what was he to do?

The rain fell and the wind blew and the gutters filled with water and became little streams.

Many people passed along the street, but no one noticed the tin soldier standing upside down with his bayonet caught amongst the cobbles.

Only a little dog saw him and barked.

"Stop fussing, Flash," called the dog's master, dragging him quickly onwards. "We can't loiter about in this rain. This is the weather to hurry home to our warm fireside."

The little tin soldier felt tears welling up in his eyes, but he did not let them fall.

How he would love to be by the warm

fireside in the playroom. How he longed to glimpse the beautiful dancer standing gracefully on her one leg.

He would not be hurt by the jeering remarks of the Jack-in-the box if only he could be back in the safety of the playroom.

The toy soldier set his face firmly in a brave expression and did not complain. He knew that he must be steadfast like a true soldier and not allow himself to be depressed by his difficult situation.

To make the time pass, the little tin soldier thought about all his favourite things: the beautiful dancer, the crackle of logs on the playroom fire, the smell of freshly-baked bread, the springtime cherry blossom in the garden and the rainbow he had seen after a shower.

11

It seemed that the tin soldier stood in the gutter for hours, but at last the rain stopped falling and two boys came skipping along the pavement.

Their sharp, young eyes saw the tin soldier and they picked him up.

"Here's a stout-hearted fellow," they smiled.

"I wonder how he came to be out here?" said one.

"Goodness knows!" replied the other. "But he deserves a treat after standing in all this rain." Then they noticed that the tin soldier had only one leg.

"Well, he is a brave fellow to stand so well to attention and to hold that heavy musket so firmly on his shoulder," they decided.

"What is your name and where do you live?" they asked. "Are you very far from your home?"

"We will take you there if you will only speak and tell us where to go," they said, for they were kind-hearted boys.

How the tin soldier longed to tell them about the warm playroom along the road, but the cold had frozen his lips and he could not say a word.

He could only stand straight and firm, like a true soldier.

"Well, if you cannot tell us where you live, then we will keep you," smiled the boys, who had taken quite a fancy to the brave little chap.

One of the lads held the tin soldier in his hands and they walked away along the road, pleased that they had spotted him.

If the tin soldier had stayed with the lads he would have had a happy home, but the wicked, magical Jack-in-the-box was still casting his evil spells in the direction of the little tin soldier.

Through his magic, the Jack-in-the-box could see that the tin soldier had been rescued. He sent thoughts to lodge in the heads of the boys, who had no idea that they were being influenced by such a strange, hard-hearted mischief-maker.

The boys looked at the streams still running along the gutters. "Let us give the soldier a ride in a boat" suggested one of the boys. "It will be a treat for him. He cannot have travelled about much in the past with only one leg."

"Good idea!" agreed the other.

He pulled some paper from his pocket and started to fold it into a boat-shape.

The rainwater was still running swiftly along the gutters in a wide stream.

One of the boys held up the soldier and spoke to him.

"Have you ever been on a boat trip before?" he asked. "It is fine fun. You can pretend you are a soldier being sent to foreign parts to fight the enemies of the king. Pirates will attack you and foreign fighting ships will chase you. You will be caught in storms and lost in fog, but you will battle through and your country will be proud of you."

The steadfast tin soldier stood to attention.

This boat trip sounded full of adventure. He would face up to it as a brave soldier should.

"The boat is ready now," called the boy who had been folding the paper.

They stood the tin soldier in the paper boat and set it sailing on the water swirling down the edge of the road.

It was indeed an extremely perilous trip.

The boat swayed from side to side. It raced round corners and was almost wrecked on some jagged cobbles.

Through all the dangers the little tin soldier stood up straight and tall and showed no fear, but kept his brave face looking forward, as a soldier should.

The boys ran after him.

"This is the best fun we have had in weeks," they laughed.

"What a grand soldier and what a fine boat!" they chuckled.

The tin soldier did indeed feel that he was in a handsome boat sailing to foreign lands in search of adventure.

"If only the lovely dancer were sailing with me, I should be completely happy," he thought.

But the dancer was not with him and the magical Jack-in-the-box was still plotting for mischief to befall.

The merry, bubbling stream flowing along the gutter turned yet another corner.

The boys laughed and whooped and stared down at their little boat.

They did not think to look ahead. They did not see that the stream ahead was flowing under a long gutter board.

The bright, merry stream in a moment would turn into a dark, gloomy torrent with dangers hidden beneath its waves.

The boys gasped with dismay as the boat and the tin soldier swept under the gutter board and disappeared from sight.

"We seem to have lost our new toy!" they groaned. Then they cheered up.

"Perhaps the soldier will come out safely at the other *end* of the gutter board," one of the boys had suggested.

They ran along the pavement, hoping that when they reached the other end of the board they would see the little boat come sailing out with the soldier still safely aboard.

The steadfast tin soldier's heart sank as he was swept by the water into the inky blackness underneath the gutter board.

Then he brightened up.

Why, this was really no worse than being in his box back in the playroom. It was pitch dark in the box where he lived with the other soldiers, but he was never afraid. Why should this darkness be more frightening than the darkness in the box?

The brave tin soldier stood to attention and looked firmly before him and showed no fear.

Then, coming towards him, he saw a light which grew bigger and bigger. It was the light at the end of the gutter board.

Soon the soldier would be out in the air

and playing with the two nice lads again.

However, things were not to be so easy.

The mischievous Jack-in-the-box was still sending out his evil spells.

Before the little tin soldier could sail out into the sunshine a great rat which lived under the gutter board darted forward.

"Have you got a passport?" it snarled. "Where is your passport? You cannot go through here without a passport."

The rat was a fearsome sight and the little tin soldier *was* afraid, but he did not show his fear.

He kept his face firm and stood to attention and held his musket on his shoulder as a true soldier should.

The boat sailed on and the rat followed. It bared its teeth and snarled and shouted to the sticks and stones in the water to stop the soldier's boat.

"He has no passport. He has not paid a toll. Stop him. STOP HIM!"

The sticks and stones snatched at the boat. It swayed and rocked from side to side but the paper boat sailed on.

The current of the stream became stronger. The tin soldier was sure he would be overturned into the black water.

Then he heard a rushing noise. It grew into a roar and the stream flowed faster and faster. A little way before the gutter board finished, the torrent of water fell down a drain into a deep, underground canal.

Hardly had the unfortunate tin soldier realised that he would not be floating forward into the sunlight, than he fell tumbling down a long, foaming waterfall.

It was as big and dangerous to the little soldier as a drop over Niagara Falls would be to a human being.

The steadfast tin soldier bounced and tumbled and tangled with the floating rubbish and was then thrown free, only to get tangled up again.

To his great surprise, he at last found himself floating down the swirling canal. He was wet and freezing, but at least he was still in the paper boat!

"Perhaps my luck has turned," he thought. "I have certainly left that rat behind me. What an unsavoury character! Maybe the canal will take me along to somewhere pleasant and safe."

Whether the canal did indeed lead to somewhere safe and pleasant, we shall never know. The tin soldier did not get far enough to find out.

The little boat was not strong enough for such turbulent, tumbling waters.

The boat spun round and round. It filled with water. The tin solder knew it must sink soon.

He stood to attention with the water lapping up to his neck.

Then he felt the boat becoming soft and breaking up beneath him. It was only made of paper and it was being soaked to shreds.

The soldier thought of the beautiful dancer standing so gracefully on one leg. He was sure he would never again see her lovely face.

The wet paper split apart and the brave soldier slid down through the water – but not to the bottom of the canal.

Now his luck really did change, although it was hard for him to realise that it had.

As he sank down through the water, the soldier was snapped up by a big fish. How dark and narrow it was inside the fish! But then, the soldier was not afraid of the dark, so he was not too unhappy. He lay at attention, shouldering his musket and thinking brave thoughts, as a soldier should.

For a while the fish swam smoothly, then it turned and twisted and raced to and fro. Then it shot up high and fell down with a heavy slap. After that it lay still.

For a while nothing more happened.

Then the soldier saw a sudden flash of light which was dazzling to him after he had been so long in the dark.

Two fingers pulled him out from the inside of the fish and a voice said:

"A tin soldier! What a thing to find inside a fish! I must take it to show young master."

The fish had been caught and sold. A kitchen maid had cut it open to prepare it for supper and the soldier had been found in the fish's belly.

Still blinking at the sudden light, the tin soldier felt himself splashed with cold water from the tap, rubbed with a rough towel and then taken into a bright, welcoming parlour.

His eyes became accustomed to the light. As he was set on a table, he looked around him. How amazed and delighted he was to see that he was back in the very same home from which he had fallen such a long, weary time ago!

His young owner, the boy, came forward and picked him up.

"It is my own tin soldier! The one which fell out of the window," he said. "Oh, I am so pleased. I must take him along to see the other toys."

He carried the steadfast tin soldier up to the playroom. There were the other soldiers. There was the box in which the soldier lived.

Most marvellous of all – there was the lovely dancer, still balancing on one leg with her arms spread gracefully into the

air above her. The tin soldier thought he had never seen anything so lovely in all his life.

He looked round.

The Jack-in-the-box was gone.

"After all his travels, I don't think this soldier could settle down with the other soldiers again," said the boy. "He must go to live in the castle, as befits a great adventuring hero."

He put the soldier in the castle near the dancer and then he went away to supper.

After that, the happy boy would go to bed.

Later on the toys came to life, as usual. They asked to hear the soldier's story. They told him the Jack-in-the-box had been thrown away as a result of all his naughtiness.

Most agreeable of all, the dancer smiled and danced round the soldier and said that as he was now a great man and had been so brave, she would marry him and they could live in the castle. And they lived happily ever after.

The Green Dragon

As all of us who have lived long enough will know, weather can change.

For years the winters in a country can be mild, with scarcely any snow. No one has any trouble travelling on the roads. Ordinary clothes keep folk quite warm.

The old people – or even the middle-aged people say: "The winters *can* be bad. I remember when the roads were three feet deep with snow. I remember when the water froze in the pipes. I remember when we could not get up to that palace on the mountain top for three months."

The young people would look at each other and smile.

"It couldn't possibly have been as bad as that," they would say to each other. "Those old folk are exaggerating to make a good story."

Then the old folk – or the middle-aged folk – would say: "We can remember when we had to wear long woolly underwear with thick shirts and jumpers and trousers on top of that and overcoats and scarves and gloves and still we were not warm enough – and that was indoors in front of a blazing fire!"

Again the young people would snigger and think: "What softies the old folk must have been when they were young. Why, we only wear short cotton underwear and thin jumpers and trousers. Those old folk should have eaten proper food and taken enough exercise and then they would have been warm enough."

Then suddenly, after all the years of mild weather – WHOOSH!

A bad winter comes.

It becomes colder than usual and the snowflakes drift across the land. More snow falls. Icy winds blow. Roads are blocked. Water freezes in the pipes. People wear so many clothes they can hardly move – and still they are cold.

Then the old folk and the middle-aged folk say: "There you are. We told you so!"

The young people say: "This must be the worst weather ever. It was never as bad as this before. It must all be the fault of cutting down too much forest or catching too many fish. Something should be done."

But whatever anyone says, the bad weather has arrived and everyone has to put up with it.

Except once, in one country, a young fellow called Lysander did not feel like putting up with the bad weather.

He was especially annoyed because his lady love, Matilda, lived in a castle on top of a mountain and the roads to the castle were blocked by snow.

Instead of sitting down and shivering, Lysander stood up and thought.

He wondered about a dragon in a far country, who breathed fire and flame and was feared by all. "He is the very chap we need here," said Lysander and he travelled to the far country.

"You must be very lonely if you are feared by all," said Lysander to the dragon. "It must be miserable if everyone runs away every time you stop for a chat."

The dragon had to agree.

"If you come to my country you will be welcome and everyone will be pleased to see you," said Lysander, "and what is more we have a good supply of that brimstone you enjoy eating."

With no more ado, the dragon went with Lysander to his country. He breathed fire and flame with every step. He cleared the snow from the valleys. Then he cleared the roads to the castle where Matilda lived.

Everyone was happy.

When Lysander was old, the bad weather came again. The dragon had left and no one believed Lysander's way to make life better. So the people stayed cold!

The Enchanted Patches

Hundreds of years ago, the world was a very different place.

Some people say that there was magic in those days, and witches and fairies and enchantment. Perhaps there was and perhaps there was not.

A girl called Esmerelda did not know much about it either way.

She lived in the country and life was hard. Esmerelda was always far too busy working to have time to think about such a thing as magic.

If she heard the other girls talking about magicians or magic wishes while they were helping weed the vegetable patch, Esmerelda would say: "If you ever meet a magician, send him round here to pull up the weeds."

But no magician ever came a-calling at Esmerelda's cottage.

When at last a magician did arrive, Esmerelda did not recognize him.

In those days there were no comfortable restaurants nor cafés dotted along the roads. The muddy footpaths wound on for mile after mile, through the quiet and lonely countryside.

The people living in monasteries and big castles and even humble cottages were supposed to let travellers sleep in their woodsheds or barns, and kind people put out simple food and drink for folk who were walking along the road.

So Esmerelda did not think it strange when an old man in rags came trudging along her garden path and asked if he could sleep in the cowshed for the night, and if she could spare him a drink of clean water and some bread and cheese.

She agreed and as she had had a fairly easy day herself, with the vegetables all freshly picked and a friend having come to help milk the cows, Esmerelda even offered to patch the old man's coat for him where the patches were odd.

He was pleased and grateful, and sat by the fire chatting while Esmerelda took all the odd coloured patches from his clothes and replaced them with material which matched the coat.

Then he went to sleep in the cowshed and before Esmerelda woke the next morning, he went on his way.

She tidied the cottage and she picked up the patches she had taken from the old man's coat. She sighed: "How I wish I had some beautiful clothes."

At once a big chest appeared. Esmerelda opened it and saw that it was filled with lovely dresses, all her size. She was very surprised. It was the first time a wish of hers had ever been granted.

Then Esmerelda noticed that one of the patches from the old man's coat had disappeared.

Esmerelda was no fool. She realized at once that magic was at work and thought: "These patches must each grant a wish."

Holding another of the coloured pieces of cloth, Esmerelda wished that the old man was back in the cottage.

The old man appeared at once, but Esmerelda hardly recognized him, he looked so well-dressed.

"Why have you brought me back here?" he asked.

"Well," replied Esmerelda, "you left these patches behind and they grant wishes so it seemed only right that I should share the wishes with you."

"What an honest girl you are!" said the man. "Most people would have used the wishes and not bothered about fetching me. I left the patches on purpose to grant you some nice wishes because you were so kind to me. Now I see how honest you are, I will grant you another wish. It is that the patches will bring you happiness. Now go ahead and use the patches for whatever else you desire."

Esmerelda took another patch in her hand and wished that her home should become a beautiful palace – and it did.

"Very wise," agreed the old man. "A fine roof over her head always seems to make a young lady look more beautiful."

Esmerelda took another patch in her hand and wished the palace should have enough servants to keep it in good condition with their wages paid for ever.

"You are sensible," said the old man. "Would you think of taking a husband?"

Esmerelda blushed and nodded her head.

"Good," smiled the old man. "I am a magician, but I have a human son and he is out hunting somewhere near here. He is a handsome boy, but a little wild at times. I'm sure if he married you he would settle down and do very well."

So Esmerelda used the last patch to wish that she and the old man's son should fall in love and marry, which they did.

And they lived happily ever after.

Why Humpty Dumpty Fell off the Wall

Humpty Dumpty sat on a wall. Humpty Dumpty had a great fall. All the king's horses and all the king's men could not put Humpty together again.

"I'm not surprised," said the queen. "They are going about things in quite the wrong way."

The king liked Humpty Dumpty. Humpty could always be relied on to call out jolly remarks as he sat on the wall. And as he sat on the wall most of the day, he saw all the comings and goings and who called on whom and who got up early and who came home late.

He told the king lots of gossip and was a very useful chap.

The king sent away all his horses and all his men. He turned to the queen.

"If you can make Humpty Dumpty better, please do so," he said.

Humpty Dumpty was rather an odd-looking fellow. No one was ever sure whether he was an egg which looked like a human being, or a human who was so

fat and bald that he looked like an egg.

At the moment he looked very poorly as he lay on the ground with his clothes dirty and torn and his shell or skin, whichever the case might be, cracked and scratched. The queen called her ladies-in-waiting and her servants.

They measured Humpty Dumpty's clothes and made new clothes to fit him. They covered his scratches and wounds with sticky, gluey ointment.

"If he is human, that will heal his skin. If he is an egg, it will glue his shell together," smiled the queen.

After a few weeks, Humpty Dumpty was quite well and feeling his old self again.

"Thank you, Your Majesty," he said to

the queen, thinking that now he could go back to sitting on the wall. But poor old Humpty Dumpty was in for a big surprise.

The queen was the sort of person who liked to give advice to people.

"Your trouble, Mr. Dumpty," said the queen, "is that you spend too much time sitting on that wall and not enough time taking exercise. That is why you fell off. You were not fit. You were out of condition. From now on you must spend two hours a day dancing. It will do you good."

Poor Humpty! He had never taken any exercise in his life before. However, when he tried it, he found that he *liked* dancing. He became so healthy and busy that he never had time to sit on the wall!

27

The Perfect Knight

Once upon a time there lived a knight called Sir Galahad. He was a perfect, gentle knight.

He was brave and honest and kind and true. Everyone liked him. Everyone admired him.

Sometimes, when a person is good and perfect, other people are jealous of them and hate them.

This was not the case with Sir Galahad. He was so pleasant and well-meaning and dependable that no one could ever say a bad word about him.

Now, it is very unusual for anyone to be as perfect as was Sir Galahad.

Legends and stories grew up about him.

Some folk said Sir Galahad was so good himself that he had only to look at another person to sense whether that person was honest or a cheat.

Other folk said that Sir Galahad was so truthful that if anyone stood near him who had ever told a lie, that person would turn bright red from shame.

None of this was true at all. Sir Galahad was such a nice fellow, he would never have dreamed of upsetting anyone by making them seem bad in any way.

However, people *believed* that the stories were true and when word got about that Sir Galahad was to visit a town called Blazing Sun, the folk who lived there became nervous.

To start with the name of the town was very misleading. The sun did not blaze down on it the whole time.

The townsfolk had put a picture of the sun over the town gateway and called the town Blazing Sun, because they hoped the talk of sunshine would attract a lot of visitors.

If the sun did not shine and the rain fell while Sir Galahad was visiting, the townsfolk would feel rather embarrassed, but anyway, the day came when he rode on his horse through the town gateway.

If you look at the picture you will see the townsfolk hiding and peeping so that they could see Sir Galahad, but he could not see them.

There is a man under the bridge, a man in a barrel, a man peering from an open doorway, a man with a sword pretending to be a statue, a young lady pretending to be part of a stained glass window, a man on a roof and a man in the shadows of the gateway.

It was not that these people were bad. It was that they were not perfect and did not wish to be shown up by this famous knight.

Clip-clop! Clip-clop!

Sir Galahad rode into town.

"Do come out and speak to me," he called. "It will make me so happy to talk to you lovely people."

When they heard such a pretty speech all the townsfolk came out of hiding.

When they saw that no one turned red nor was accused by Sir Galahad of being a cheat, they relaxed and were happy and enjoyed the visit.

Sir Galahad said they were all beautiful, wonderful, warm-hearted folk and they *loved* him.

The town even lived up to its name of Blazing Sun.

As Sir Galahad left, the mayor said to him: "We are so pleased it did not rain during your visit and spoil the reputation of our fair town."

"Oh, you need not have worried about that," smiled Sir Galahad. "Everyone here has such a sunny smile that had it rained, I really would not have noticed!"

So none of them need have been worried about Sir Galahad's visit at all.

❀ The Swan Queen ❀

This is the story of two good and brave children. Their names were Maria and Carl and their strange adventure took them to the throne of the Swan Queen.

The tale starts a little while ago, not *very* long ago, just a little while – about as long ago as a Grandma might just be able to remember if she tried very hard.

Maria and Carl dwelt in a country called Bavaria. They were not poor. They were not rich.

They lived on a small farm with their mother and father. If they all worked fairly hard and the weather was kind, they had plenty to eat and could afford new clothes every Easter.

If the weather was unkind and the family took too many days off to visit Auntie Hannah over the hill, or Grandma down in the village, then sometimes the children could not spread as much butter on their bread as they would have liked.

However, on the whole life was good.

The children had to help with the farm work, but all children helped with their families' tasks in those days.

Schools closed down at harvest time so that whole families could go into the fields together and gather in all the crops before the weather turned cold.

Then, one year, life stopped being so pleasant for Maria and Carl. They were out in the sunny fields helping to harvest the wheat, when Maria noticed that Mummy was looking very ill.

"Daddy!" called Maria. "Mummy is not well."

They all stopped work and gathered round Mummy.

"It's nothing much," she said. "I think the hot sun must be too strong on my head. I will rest in the shade for a little while."

The others did Mummy's share of the work while she rested.

Daddy helped her home at the end of the day. The good and clever children prepared supper, so that Mummy could go to bed and do no more work.

They all thought that by the next morning Mummy would be better.

She was not.

It was so unusual for Mummy to be ill.

It was even more unusual for her to make any fuss about it.

Even when she had quite a bad cold, Mummy usually said: "Oh, I will get up. I hate staying in bed. I shall feel better if I am up and about."

This time Mummy lay in bed.

She ate very little. She always appeared to have a fever. She seemed to lose interest in everything.

When the children came to see her in the evening, she did not bother to ask them about the little things they had been doing.

It was all rather frightening and not like Mummy at all.

"I am afraid your mother is very ill," Daddy said to Maria and Carl.

The children knew he was right.

The doctor came to the house and shook his head and went away.

"I cannot cure your mother's sickness," he sighed. "She is beyond medicines."

Maria had to stay at home and do the cooking. She did it very well, but no one could enjoy their food very much when they knew Mummy was lying ill upstairs.

Then one day Carl came running into the kitchen. He looked happy and cheery.

Maria stared at him in surprise.

"Good news!" puffed Carl. "I have been talking to those boys who live on the other side of the hill. One of their pigs got out and was running wild in the woods and they were out looking for him. Anyway, they asked how we all were and I told them about Mummy. And they said they had an

auntie who was ill with just the same sort of thing and her children went to see the wise woman on the hill and she told them how to cure the illness and everything was fine."

"How wonderful!" smiled Maria. "Did you ask exactly where this wise woman lives?"

"I certainly did," smiled Carl, "and I think we should go to see her tomorrow morning."

The next day the children set out.

It was a steep climb to reach the home of the wise woman on the hill. Bavaria is a mountainous country and what the folk there call a hill is much steeper and higher than hills in some other lands.

By the time Maria and Carl reached the broken, rotting wooden steps which led up to the home of the wise woman, they were tired.

At the sound of the children's approach, two fierce black dogs came snarling and yelping through the open front doorway.

Maria clutched at Carl.

"I am afraid to go up there," she said. "Those dogs will bite us and the house is dark and very odd. Are you sure this is the right place?"

"Yes, I'm sure," replied Carl. "And an old lady living alone up here is bound to have fierce dogs to guard her home. If we call out and say we mean no harm, we shall get in to see her safely."

Carl called out in his very loudest voice:

"Wise woman! Wise woman! We want to talk to you about something very important. Please call off your dogs and let us come in and speak to you."

An old lady came and stood in the doorway and looked down the steps. When she saw her visitors were merely two children, she told the dogs to sit quietly and invited the children indoors.

Carl and Maria climbed cautiously up the old wooden steps. They were afraid of falling through the rotting planks and hurting themselves.

"If she is so wise, why can't she keep her steps in good repair?" muttered Maria.

"Shshshsh!" hissed Carl. "She might hear you and be cross with us."

Inside, the house was rather bare but quite clean and the wise woman had a kindly expression.

The children told her all about their mother's illness: how she had felt faint out in the field and later, how she had lain listlessly in bed with flushed cheeks and had eaten hardly anything.

The wise woman looked serious.

"Does she cough much?" she asked.

"Yes," replied Marie. "Do you know what

maybe wrong? Can you help our mother?"

"I do know what is wrong," replied the wise old woman, "and I can help but I have no medicine which will cure your mother's illness. The berries and leaves from which it must be made will not grow on this hill. However, I can tell you where to go to find the medicine your mother needs."

The children were so happy.

"Where?" they laughed. "Where must we go? Tell us and we will start out at once."

"Not so fast!" sighed the wise woman. "It is a long way and not an easy one. You will have to keep your wits about you or you will not be let through. In any case you must first go home and tell your father what you are about to do."

The children promised to go home and prepare properly for their journey and then the wise woman gave them instructions for the start of their adventure. They were smiling when they said goodbye to her.

Maria and Carl went home to speak to their father. They explained to him about their visit to the wise woman.

"She told us that we can get the medicine Mother needs from the Swan Queen," said Carl "but to reach the Swan Queen we have to go on quite a long journey. We must start by going through a tunnel at the foot

breakfast, for they did not know when they would eat their next meal.

They walked to the foot of the White Mountain. As the wise woman had said they would, they found a cave.

Bravely they walked in through the dark entrance. The floor was damp and slippery. The roof of the cave was uneven.

of the White Mountain. After that we must do what seems best to us. All we need take with us are our quick wits. If we use them wisely we shall be safe and successful."

The children's father was not very happy about all this. It sounded a very uncertain sort of trip. However, he was so worried about his wife and so sure that both the children were sensible that he agreed they could go.

The next morning the children ate a big

Sometimes it was high. Sometimes it came down low and the children bumped their heads.

As they went further in, the cave became dark, but as the light from the entrance faded, the children saw a tiny spot of light ahead of them.

It was the way out to the other side of the mountain.

Carl and Maria hurried on as best they could and at last went down some steps and found themselves in broad daylight.

There was no Swan Queen to be seen, but hanging on a post was a sign in the shape of a piece of jigsaw puzzle.

The children were really quite surprised. They had been expecting dragons or goblins, but not jigsaws.

"Do you think it is directing us to Jigsaw Puzzle Land?" asked Carl.

Maria looked around.

"There is no other road and no other signpost," she said. "That is the way we have to go, wherever it leads."

The weather was warm and the road was

easy. The children felt good as they walked along in the sunshine.

The road led them to a gate with a soldier guarding it.

"You cannot go through here, my young friends," he said, "not until you have joined up all those pieces of jigsaw puzzle. They must be put together correctly or you will have to go back the way you came."

The children turned and saw bits of an enormous jigsaw puzzle lying at the side of the road. The pieces were so heavy that the children could scarcely lift them. Not only that but the puzzle was not easy to understand.

"This is where we must start using our quick wits," said Carl. "I do hope it turns out that we have some!"

after a while they had completed the giant puzzle. The soldier applauded.

"Well done, youngsters!" smiled the soldier and he opened the gate and let the children through.

They hurried forward, hoping to see the Swan Queen, but they did not.

Instead, they came to a land where everything was made of jigsaw puzzles and where everyone was *doing* jigsaw puzzles.

Then they reached a sign saying: "To Nursery Rhyme Land'.

"I think we had better go on," said Carl. "Let us see if the Swan Queen is in Nursery Rhyme Land."

Carl and Maria walked a long way before they came to another gate.

It was lucky they were country children and used to walking or they would have been quite worn out.

As it was, the plucky little things were still fresh and cheery.

This second gate was also guarded by a soldier.

On the gate was a sign which read: *Today's Rhyme is 'Feasting.'*

"I cannot let you through the gate," said the soldier, "until you have thought of

Luckily, Carl and Maria were both bright little things and that big breakfast they had eaten was still giving them energy.

They worked hard and thought hard and

some sort of rhyme for the word *feasting*."

The children thought hard.

Then Maria laughed and said: "Jampot!"

"Quite right," replied the soldier and let them through.

"I did not understand that at all,"

whispered Carl, when they were safely in Nursery Rhyme Land.

"Well," smiled Maria. "I knew there must be some sort of trick in it. So I thought – what is feasting? And then I thought, why, feasting is eating a lot. And what rhymes with eating a lot – why, jampot, of course. So jampot was the answer."

Carl shook his head.

"You took a big risk, guessing like that," he said. "You could easily have been wrong."

BAAA! BAAA!

The sound of sheep bleating made the children stop chatting and look around. They certainly were in Nursery Rhyme Land. No doubt about it!

Bo-peep was walking past with her sheep. Jack Horner was pulling a plum from his pie. The pieman was going to the fair. Humpty Dumpty was sitting on the wall and the Old Woman in the Shoe was calling to her children.

"I just do not know what to do," she was saying.

"This is fun," smiled Carl. "We must try to come here again when we are not so worried about Mummy. Right now, we must go on and look for the Swan Queen."

The children walked on until they came to the edge of a wide lake. Swans were everywhere. They flew through the air, floated on the water and circled round a

tall castle which stood on an island in the middle of the lake.

Maria and Carl looked at the castle. They looked at all the swans.

"This *must* be where the Swan Queen lives," Carl exclaimed. "Thank goodness!".

Maria nodded.

"We are almost there," she said, "but how shall we get to the island?"

For a while the children walked along

the edge of the water. Then, to their delight, they came to a ferry.

A wide, safe-looking boat with a prow shaped like a swan was tied to a little jetty. A pleasant young man sat eating an apple pie outside a pretty cottage.

He saw the children looking at the boat and then across to the castle.

"Do you want a trip on the ferry?" he asked. "I will take you across to the island for a small fee."

Fortunately, the two wise children had brought a little money with them and could have paid the fare.

However, as the young man was finishing off his apple pie, he happened to remark:

"I have a wonderful wife, but somehow she can't seem to make apple pies like mother used to make. The pastry is good, but the apples inside aren't so nice."

Maria was well-used to cooking.

"Ask your wife if she puts lemon juice and butter and sugar and cinnamon in with the apples," said Maria. "If she does that, I am sure the pies will be delicious."

The young man was very pleased with that cookery hint and in return, said he

would take the children across to the island for nothing. Which all goes to show that learning to cook properly can be very useful in unexpected ways!

The young man took the children safely across to the island.

"Give me a shout when you want to come back," he smiled. "Voices carry a long way across water. I shall hear you."

Then he was gone and the children walked up the many steps leading to the entrance of the castle.

They told the soldier on guard duty at the door that they wished to see the Swan

Queen and he took them into a huge, elegant hall.

A beautiful lady sat on a throne at the top of wide, marble steps.

She was grand and important, but she had a friendly smile.

Maria and Carl told her about their mother and her illness and how the wise woman had sent them to her, the Swan Queen.

"She did the right thing," smiled the Swan Queen. "I have the potion which will cure your mother. Come to my medicine room with me."

Carl and Maria looked at each other excitedly as they hurried along the long corridors behind the Swan Queen.

The palace seemed enormous to the two children, who had lived all their lives in a modest farmhouse. But at last, they entered a big room. Standing neatly on shelves were vast numbers of pots of different shapes and sizes, containing potions of every possible colour. The queen turned to the children and said: "This is where I keep all my medicines!"

The Swan Queen took down a bottle of greyish-white liquid.

"This is made from the berries and leaves of a plant which will only grow high up in the purest air," she explained. "My swans take me to gather them at the end of summer and before the first frosts of winter. This medicine is completely pure. It will drive out the bad, hot weather dust which your mother breathed in and which is making her suffer so much."

The Swan Queen put some of the medicine into a small bottle and gave it to Maria, who tucked it safely in a pocket.

Naturally, the children wished to go home at once and give the medicine to their mother.

They thanked the Swan Queen and turned to hurry out of the castle.

"It is late," said the Swan Queen. "Soon it will be dark. You cannot go back the way you came. It will take too long."

"What else can we do?" asked Maria. "We know no other path to reach home, except the one by which we came. The ferryman said he would fetch when we called."

"Don't worry about the ferryman," smiled the Swan Queen. "I will tell him you have gone home another way."

Then she took the children to the roof of the castle and called down two huge swans.

"These are my trusted servants," she smiled. "They will carry you safely home."

At first the children were nervous as they sat on the backs of the swans with the ground so far below. Then they saw their home ahead, and they were happy they would soon be with their mother.

Mother drank the medicine and at once she felt stronger. In a week she was better.

The whole family went to see the wise woman. They took her a present to thank her for her help.

"Do you think we should go to thank the Swan Queen?" asked Maria.

"Well now," replied the wise woman, "that is a long journey which should only be undertaken by people in great need. The swans will tell her that you are grateful, but I don't think *you* should try to go so far again. But one day, I will take you both on another visit to Nursery Rhyme Land.

The children *were* pleased. They ran to hug the old woman, who was beginning to feel like an old friend.

"You will want to spend some time with your mother, now she is well again. But we shall speak again soon," the old woman smiled.

The Royal Oak

Long ago a king lived in a fine castle on top of a hill. His was a pleasant kingdom, with warm summers and mild winters. More and more people came to live in the villages, and they rented little farms to be found in the valleys between the hills.

Now in those days people burned wood on their fires. Hardly anyone bothered with coal at all. Why should they? Coal was difficult to find and dirty to handle, while wood was lying about everywhere, just waiting to be picked up and used.

However, with so many people coming to live in the kingdom, the supply of fallen dead wood began to run out.

The farmers and villagers had to cut down living trees to get wood for their fires. The forests became smaller.

People started grumbling about how far they had to go to find wood, when in the old days it had been only a step or two from their front doors.

Then something happened which drove all thought of firewood from the people's minds.

A large band of brigands attacked the castle, threw the king and all his courtiers into prison and took over the kingdom.

Only one young prince of the royal household escaped the brigands' clutches. He had been on a hunting trip with a few companions and stayed for a night in a small hunting lodge in the forest.

Imagine their horror when they attempted to return to the castle and found strangers on guard at the gate and the signs of battle all around the walls.

The brigands were equally surprised to see the young prince and his attendants riding up to the gate of the castle.

They thought they had imprisoned all the royal family.

As soon as the young prince realized that something was dreadfully wrong and

turned to escape to the shelter of the forest, the brigands told their leader that a royal prince was at the gates.

At once the brigand chief called out a party of his soldiers and sent them after the prince to hunt him down and take him prisoner in the same way as the rest of his family had been captured.

Still confused and not really knowing what was happening, the young prince and his men ran any way they could. Soon they were separated and blundered through the trees looking for places in which to hide from the yelling brigands.

The young prince was surprised at the lack of trees behind which to take cover near the castle.

As he searched desperately for cover, he wished his father had not allowed so many trees to be cut down to supply firewood for the royal fires.

The unfortunate young prince was already tired from a morning's hunting. He knew he could not run much farther. He found himself at the foot of a mighty oak tree.

Gratefully he climbed up into its strong, thick branches and hid amongst the dense growth of leaves as the brigands ran by underneath.

He heard the sound of voices and the shouting echoing to and fro through the woodlands as the brigands called to each other in their search for him and his companions.

He became more cheerful as the sound of the voices faded into the distance, as that must have meant some of his friends were getting away.

Then more men came from the castle. Their voices were angry. They beat the undergrowth and climbed up some of the trees and yelled to each other that they must find that rascal of a prince, or they would be kept out searching all night by their tyrant of a leader.

By lucky chance they did not climb the oak tree. The prince stayed safe on his branch. He was cold and uncomfortable and he was hungry, but for the moment he was safe.

Even when night fell, the brigands came searching through the trees with flares in their hands.

Up in the oak tree the prince had to stay, glad that the branches of the tree were so wide and strong.

Some of the brigands became weary with searching and sat down to rest under the very oak in which the prince was hiding.

From their talk he learned that his family had been captured and many soldiers of the king driven out of the kingdom.

The poor boy was overcome with despair and worry.

What would become of him even if he did escape? He had no family free to help him, and the people of the kingdom would be too frightened of the brigands to give assistance.

The prince remained in the oak tree for several days. They were not pleasant days, but they could have been worse.

He drank the dew which collected on the leaves. He found stores of nuts left by squirrels. He ate berries brought to him by the birds, who had been his pets in happier days.

At last the brigands from the castle gave up looking for him.

The prince waited till darkness was falling one evening, then he dropped from the tree and walked cautiously to the farm which lay farthest from the castle and which was owned by a retired soldier from

the castle guard. Noiselessly he walked round the farmyard and through the barns, looking everywhere. Then he listened at the door of the farmhouse.

He had to make sure that no brigands were at the farm before he dared enter.

He heard nothing but the murmur of the voices of the farmer, his wife and their children.

The prince tapped at the wooden door.

The talking stopped. There was silence for several seconds.

Then the door was opened and the farmer stood outlined against the firelight.

He did not seem very surprised to see the young prince.

"I heard that they did not capture you," he said. "I thought you might come here. Come in and sit by the fire, my lord, you must be cold and hungry."

How wonderful to hear such kind words!

The prince sat by the fire and ate and drank and slept until he was over the shock of all the terrible things which had happened to his family and country.

Then the prince began to feel better.

He was young and strong and he had his life before him. He owed it to his family and his subjects to see what could be done to overthrow the brigands.

In the half-light of dusk and the early dawn, the prince walked round the kingdom. He soon learned that things were not as bad as he had thought.

His hunting companions were all safe and hiding with friends and relatives.

Some soldiers were in hiding not far from the castle.

Others had been out on duty in remote parts of the forest and were staying hidden in woodcutters' hovels or near hunting lodges, waiting for someone to tell them what to do.

The brigands living in the castle were enjoying their plunder and forgot about the careful plans they had made before they attacked and seized the castle.

They thought everyone was still so frightened of them and their fierce ways that no citizen would dare attack them.

They were raiding the richer farms for

food, but there were many parts of the forest where no brigand went for weeks on end.

The prince gathered all his soldiers and friends together in a remote part of the forest.

They built shelters and hunted freely for food. They gathered wood for their fires.

The prince went to visit other kings and came back with gifts of arms, for the neighbouring kings thought: "Let this prince defeat the brigands. If they are left to prosper, the next time they want to conquer they may be attacking *us!*"

The prince trained his little army well, and the day came when he felt they could attack the castle.

Some of the old servants still lived in the castle, now serving their new masters.

One of the young soldiers smuggled himself into the castle with some sacks of flour.

He warned the servants that the castle was to be attacked. The young soldier and the servants were clever enough to leave the little wicket gates unlocked. They succeeded in giving too much wine to the soldiers who watched the drawbridge, and did all they could to prepare for the arrival of the prince.

The young prince came storming in with his soldiers and the brigands were defeated. The king and his family and courtiers were released.

Many years passed and the prince became king and was a wise and clever ruler. He kept his castle well-guarded and posted lookouts on his borders.

No brigands succeeded in entering the kingdom while he was king. The prince – now king – thought of other things, too.

He remembered how small the forest had seemed when he had been trying to hide from the brigands and how very scarce firewood had been when he had been living in the woodlands with his soldiers.

He ordered that for every tree which was felled, two more must be planted in its place and kept well-tended.

He sent out an order to all the people, that the oak tree in which he had hidden, was never to be felled.

"I owe that tree my life," smiled the young king.

From that day on, all open-air festivities were held under the now famous oak tree.

When at last the king found the young lady he wanted to marry, he told her his story about the oak tree.

"I think that is where I would like our wedding ceremony to take place," she said.

The king was delighted and after the wedding the tree was named by everybody The Royal Oak.

The Fairy Garden

Once upon a time, a little while ago, not as far back as when dragons and fairies lived, but about the time when Grandpa was a lad, there lived two neighbours.

They were called Mr. Greenfingers and Mr. Growfine.

Mr. Greenfingers and Mr. Growfine were very keen on gardening.

Their lawns were green and smooth. Their flowers were bright and beautiful.

In their gardens, weeds were pulled up and thrown away the moment they dared to show their heads.

The two men were really good friends. They had so much in common. They would lean over the fence between their gardens and talk about how the weather was too dry or how the weather was too wet.

The weather was always *too* something, you could be sure of that.

Or they would talk about how there were too many greenfly or would the late frosts spoil the apple blossom.

On and on they would chat about gardening, never running out of things to say and never feeling that anything else was important.

Everyone else could be yawning their heads off at hearing for the tenth time how the cold wind was holding back the daffodils. Mr. Greenfingers and Mr. Growfine could go on talking about these things for hours.

It seemed that two people could never be better friends.

Then one day something happened to spoil the cosy friendship.

A herald from the king rode round the streets.

"Hear this! Hear this!" he shouted. "His Royal Highness, King Albert, is searching for a new royal gardener. He is looking for the best gardener in the whole kingdom. In three months time the king will send inspectors to look at every garden in the land.

"Whichever man has kept the best garden, that man will be made the new royal gardener.

"The royal gardener has a hundred men to help him do the work. He has free clothes, free food, a free house and a big bag of gold at the end of every year as wages."

Then the herald rode away to say the same thing again in the next village.

Mr. Greenfingers thought to himself: "I should like to be the new royal gardener. I am such a clever fellow that really this little garden of mine is not big enough to show what I can do. I will be the royal gardener so that the whole kingdom can enjoy the beautiful display of flowers that only *I* am clever enough to make in the royal gardens. And that bag of gold will be very nice, too."

Now, unfortunately, Mr. Growfine was thinking exactly the same thoughts.

At once, each set to work even harder in his garden, so that in three months' time he would have the finest garden in the land.

Each was so busy that for a few weeks they did not speak to each other and did not notice what the other was doing.

Then Mr. Greenfingers saw how lovely the garden of Mr. Growfine was looking. It was better than his own.

"This will never do," he thought and snipped off one of Mr. Growfine's finest flowers.

Of course, you can imagine how Mr. Growfine felt when he saw that!

Mr. Growfine was furious. "Stop that, you wretch," he shouted.

Naturally Mr. Growfine was furious at these words.

He roared with rage and leaping over the fence between the two gardens, he tore a branch from Mr. Greenfingers' finest apple tree.

"How disgraceful! How can anyone be so selfish and petty and small-minded?" shrieked Mr. Greenfingers.

He jumped into the garden of Mr. Growfine and broke the glass in Mr. Growfine's cucumber frame.

Had Mr. Growfine noticed this, he would not have been pleased.

"Now do be reasonable," replied Mr. Greenfingers. "Everyone knows I am the best gardener in the land and deserve to become the next royal gardener. If by some silly chance, your garden happens to be looking better than mine, then it is only right that your garden should be – er – helped down a peg or two – so that my garden will look the best, as is only right and proper."

However, he was busily digging a furrow across Mr. Greenfingers' smooth green lawn.

The two men fell into a fine fury. Seeing their beautiful gardens damaged was, of course, enough to make them cross, but they were also driven on by greed, the desire for the grand job of royal gardener and for those yearly bags of gold.

It was unfortunate that just as the gardens were at their worst and Mr. Greenfingers and Mr. Growfine were red with rage, the king rode by.

"Stop all this quarrelling," he ordered. "I will not have such behaviour in my land.

And how you have time to quarrel when your gardens are such a disgrace, I do not know. I have never seen such untidy land!"

The king's words made the two men realize what they were doing. Neither of them would be given the post of royal gardener now.

They stopped shouting and wrecking and destroying. They helped each other to put right all the damage. In fact they took down the fence between their gardens and made one big garden.

This was when the fairies who are said to live at the bottom of every garden came to their aid. Overnight they planted beautiful flowers in the huge garden.

The next day the king happened to be passing by and you can imagine his surprise when he saw the fairy garden.

He made both Mr. Greenfingers and Mr. Growfine royal gardeners, which pleased them very much. When one was feeling a little lazy, the other could do the work, until the first one felt energetic again. This made the fairies very happy.

The two friends had found that life was easier if they both worked together rather than if they always argued.

The Rainmaker

Once upon a time, in a faraway land there lived a very wise old man. He had met hundreds of people and watched and remembered everything.

The wise old man lived in a hut outside a country village. He liked to be away from the village. It was quieter.

When you are young, you like lots of company and friends dropping in and eating meals with you and having a dance or a chat.

When you get older you begin to think that visitors make a lot of washing up and that every visitor to the house is one more pair of muddy shoes tramping across your nice clean floor.

So the old man was happy to live quietly, growing the small amount of food he needed and keeping a few chickens and a goat.

Then one year the dry weather went on for too long.

"If we do not get some rain soon our crops will be spoiled," thought the villagers.

The wise old man was not worried. He had built a small pond where a stream ran through a cave in the hills and he had his own little supply of water and his crops were growing well.

He was not called wise for nothing.

The villagers spoke amongst themselves about him and said: "That wise old man is supposed to have sat at the feet of the magicians of old, when he was a lad. Do you think he knows the Dance of the Rainmakers?"

There was only one way to find out, and two of the villagers went to the old man on the outskirts of the village and asked him if he could perform the Dance of the Rainmakers.

"Yes, I did learn the dance when I was young," replied the wise old man. "Would you like me to do it for you?"

"Yes, please," replied the two villagers. "Our crops are dying for lack of rain."

So the wise old man, who was actually quite pleased at being asked to do such an important thing, went to the top of one of the hills overlooking the village and performed the Rain Dance.

This was no easy task.

The old man had to shout over and over again, in his loudest voice, these words:

"God of the Rain. God of the Wind. Lord of the Lightning and the Thunder. Listen to me. Come when I call. Suck up the water. Carry it here. Crash with your thunder. Flash fire with your lightning. POUR DOWN THE RAIN FROM THE SKY!"

He had to remember all that, in the right order – which was not easy – and keep shouting it and waving his arms and stamping his feet, until the rain fell.

It was all very difficult and extremely tiring and meant that for days afterwards the poor old man had a very sore throat.

However, the wise old man felt sorry for the villagers and he did the Rain Dance and shouted the Rain Chant, until at last the rain fell.

"Thank you," shouted the two villagers, turning round and running for home as the rain came pouring down.

After a day, the rain stopped falling, which was just what the wise old man had intended. He had shouted long enough to get sufficient rain to do the crops good, but

Dance," he croaked in a voice which was still squeaky from the Rain Chant.

The village women grinned.

The wise old man went to find the two villagers who had come to ask him to do the Dance of the Rainmakers.

"You believe I caused the rain to fall, don't you?" he asked.

They hesitated before answering him and then said. "It would probably have rained anyway. "We only asked you because anything was worth a try."

The wise old man thought of his sore throat and how his arms and legs ached from all that waving and stamping.

He was furious with the village people. "I will teach you whether I can make rain or not," he shouted.

He ran back to the top of the hill and did the Rain Dance for a night and a day. Gradually, the clouds gathered. Then the lightning flashed and the rain fell.

The rain went on falling until the village was badly flooded and some of it almost washed away.

The village folk came pleading with the old man to stop the rain.

"Do you believe I *can* stop and start the rain?" he asked.

"Oh yes. *Yes*. We do. We *do*," they said.

So the wise old man, who was quite kind-

not enough rain to spoil them.

Now the wise old man was only human and he thought the village folk would admire him very much.

"I'm sure they are saying how wonderfully clever I am," he thought. "I think, just for once, I will take a stroll into the village to hear the folk saying kindly things about me."

The wise old man went for a walk along the village street.

To his surprise, no one took very much notice of him.

At last he said to one of the women doing her washing in the newly-flowing stream. "Don't you think it was very clever of me to make that rain fall? You could not be doing that washing now if I had not performed the Rain Dance and made water flow in that stream."

"All right, grandad, if you say so," she grinned cheekily. "I don't believe in all that mumbo-jumbo myself. I think it would have rained anyway, but if you like to feel big-headed because you jumped up and down on top of that hill and then it started to rain, good luck to you. I'm not one to spoil anyone's fun."

The wise old man was very cross.

"The rain fell because I did my Rain

hearted when people did not offend him, stopped the rain, even though it gave him another sore throat for two or three weeks, and the village was a happy place again.

Some of the most sensible of the young folk fell into the habit of visiting the wise old man and asking him to teach them chants and dances and wise sayings and clever secrets. The chant and dance that all of them wanted to know how to do was the one that brought the rain. Then they remembered they would have to learn the chant and dance to stop it.

The old man did teach them the things that he had learned. For the wise old man was human and it was very nice to have a circle of young folk sitting in front of him telling him how very clever he was.